THE BODLEY HEAD
London

Don't forget the bacon!
Pat Hutchins

OTHER PICTURE BOOKS
BY PAT HUTCHINS

Changes, Changes
Clocks and More Clocks
The Doorbell Rang
Good-Night, Owl!
Happy Birthday, Sam
King Henry's Palace
One-Eyed Jake
One Hunter · Rosie's Walk
The Silver Christmas Tree
The Surprise Party
Titch · Tom and Sam
The Very Worst Monster
Where's the Baby?
The Wind Blew
You'll Soon Grow into Them, Titch

Copyright © 1976 by Pat Hutchins
ISBN 0–370–11542–2
Printed in Great Britain for
The Bodley Head Children's Books
32 Bedford Square, London WC1B 3SG
by Cambus Litho, East Kilbride
Published in New York by Greenwillow Books, 1976
First published in Great Britain 1976
Reprinted 1979, 1982, 1984, 1987, 1989

For Ben and Jeb Kidd

41 The Cake Shop 41

fresh cream cakes

41